This book belongs to

Michael Tyler   9/30/96

WENDY'S
ADVENTURE IN NEVER LAND

WALT DISNEY FUN-TO-READ LIBRARY

ISBN 1-885222-21-1
Advance Publishers Inc., P.O. Box 2607, Winter Park, FL. 32790
Printed in the United States of America
098765432

Wendy and her brothers, John and Michael, were having a great pillow fight.

"Oh, Michael, John! Stop! The room is
full of feathers!" cried Wendy.

Just then, in came their mother and father. "My goodness! What a mess," said their mother.

"You are all too old to play such games," said their father. "Isn't that right, Nana?"

Nana wagged her tail. She tried her best to look stern.

"Now hop into bed and get some sleep," said their mother. "Remember, tomorrow is Michael's birthday."

Their mother and father and Nana kissed them each good night. They closed the door behind them as they left.

"I don't care what they say. I won't grow up if we can't have pillow fights," said Michael.
"Grown-ups never have any fun," said John. "I won't grow up either—so there!"

"Neither will I!" said Wendy. She thought for a moment. "Wait! I have an idea!" she cried. "If we go to live in Never Land with Peter Pan, we won't have to grow up! Not ever."

"What a wonderful idea!" said the boys.

"I wish Peter Pan were here," Wendy said softly.

Peter Pan was the boy who never grew up. He lived in Never Land. With him lived his band of Lost Boys and the pixie, Tinker Bell. Peter heard Wendy's wish and flew to her window.

Wendy and the boys told Peter their plan.
"Of course I'll take you back to Never
Land," said Peter Pan. "Then you won't ever
have to grow up! Just a bit of pixie dust and
off we go!"

At last they all reached Never Land. Wendy and her brothers were glad to be back.

"It's Wendy! Hurray!" shouted the Lost Boys.

Everyone was happy but tiny Tinker Bell. "What a fuss over Wendy and her brothers," she said.

"Oh boy, I can't wait until tomorrow. It's my birthday! I bet you have really wonderful birthday parties in Never Land, don't you?" asked Michael.

"Birthday parties?" asked the Lost Boys. "What are they?"

"We have birthday parties every year, for each year that we grow older," said John.

"We have cake and candles," said Michael.

"Balloons and costumes—"

"And lots of presents!"

"We <u>never</u> have birthday parties here," said Peter. "We don't grow older."

"No birthday parties!" gasped Wendy, John, and Michael.

"No," said Peter. "But we make up for that. We have fun every day of the year!"

"That's right!" shouted the Lost Boys.
"We get up at any time we like—"
"No one tells us to wash our hands or comb our hair—"
All the boys talked at once.
John and Michael cheered up right away.
But Wendy did not look happy.

"Come on, Wendy," said Peter Pan. "Let's take a walk. When you remember how beautiful Never Land is, you will forget all about birthday parties."

Tinker Bell watched Peter and Wendy.
She was not very happy about Wendy living
in Never Land.

As Wendy and Peter sat by the beach, a rowboat came up to shore. In the boat were Captain Hook and his faithful pirate, Smee! They climbed out of the boat. They crept behind the bushes. There they could hear what Peter and Wendy were saying.

"Birthday parties are important, Peter. At ours we had wonderful cakes. There were presents for everyone," they heard Wendy say.

"I like the sound of birthday parties, Smee," said Captain Hook. "I must have one. We have to capture Wendy. I want her to give a birthday party for <u>me</u>!"

"I have an idea, Wendy," cried Peter. "We'll give you and your brothers a welcoming party. It won't be the same as a birthday party. But it will be lots of fun!" Peter ran to tell the boys.

"I am going to look for some berries,"
said Wendy. "I'll make some special party
pies." Off she went into the woods.

"Aha!" said Captain Hook. "Now is our chance! Let's get her!" He and Smee grabbed Wendy and ran.

Tinker Bell saw the pirates carry Wendy away. "Good," she thought. "Now I must make sure no one finds out what has happened. Peter will soon forget about Wendy and that silly party!" Quickly she flew over the boys. She sprinkled them with pixie dust.

The boys went right to sleep. Not one of them heard Wendy's cries for help.

John and Michael were the first ones to wake up.

"Goodness," said John, "Never Land really is different. We don't have to go to bed to fall asleep."

"Where is Wendy?" asked Michael.

All the boys looked for Wendy. They could not find her anywhere.
Michael began to cry.

Tinker Bell heard Michael cry. "Oh dear,"
she thought. "I didn't want the boys to cry.
I had better make sure that Wendy is all
right, before it is too late."

Captain Hook and Smee were about to put Wendy into their boat.

"No, no, no! I won't give you a party," cried Wendy. "Let me go, you wicked creatures! Let me go!"

Faster than a butterfly, Tinker Bell flew back to Peter Pan and the boys.

"Tink has found Wendy," said Peter. "Captain Hook and Smee have her! Captain Hook wants Wendy to give him a birthday party."

"We've got to save her," cried John.
"But how?" asked the Lost Boys.
Peter thought for a moment. Then he came up with a plan.

"Captain Hook wants a party," said Peter. "So we'll just give him one. Didn't Wendy say that sometimes people wear costumes to parties?" he asked.

"Yes," said Michael. "Silly costumes or scary costumes."

"Then that is what we will do. There is
no time to waste. We'll all switch clothes and
wear twigs and branches. That will surprise
Hook and Smee all right!" said Peter.
     They all changed quickly.
     "Come on, everyone. Let's get them!"
cried Peter.

Tinker Bell led them through the woods. They came to the beach and jumped out from behind the trees.

Hook and Smee gasped in surprise. Who were these strange creatures?

"Surprise!" shouted Peter and the boys. "Drats, it's Peter Pan! I should have known," groaned Captain Hook. He lifted Wendy. "You're coming with me, little girl."

Peter tripped Captain Hook. Down went Hook. Up flew Wendy. But she landed safely in Peter's arms.

Hook and Smee ran quickly to their rowboat.

"After them!" cried the Lost Boys.

"Oh, let them go. Wendy is safe," said Peter. "It is punishment enough that Hook will never have a party."

Hook and Smee rowed away fast. "I'll get you yet, Peter Pan. Just wait and see!" shouted Hook.

"They're gone!" yelled the boys. "Hurray!"
"Thank goodness," said Wendy.
"And don't come back!" shouted Peter.
"I don't think they'll be back for a while,"
said Wendy. She pointed to the water.

They all saw the crocodile swimming after Captain Hook. They laughed and headed back through the woods.

"I want to go home," said Michael in a small voice. "I want a <u>real</u> birthday party with Mom and Dad and Nana."

"I would like to go home too," said John. "Just think how unhappy they would be if we really stayed away forever."

Wendy smiled at her brothers. "Maybe growing up won't be so bad after all," she said.

Peter Pan was sorry to see Wendy and the boys go. But Tinker Bell sprinkled them all with pixie dust so they could not change their minds.

Then she and Peter flew them home.

Wendy tucked her sleepy brothers into bed. Then she went to the window.

"Good-bye, Peter Pan and Tinker Bell," she said. "Someday we will see you again. Even though we grow up, part of us will never <u>really</u> grow up all the way."